MORTIMER'S CROSS

'And what about Mortimer? He's ever so quiet. That's never a good sign, you know it isn't. I only hope he's not up to something.'

Mr Jones hoped so too. He knew that when Mortimer was quiet, it did often mean that he was thoughtfully pecking at the gas boiler, or dropping eggs off the top of the wardrobe to see how many bounced, or pouring weedkiller into the television . . .

Another chaotic and fun-filled adventure for the Jackanory favourites – Arabel and Mortimer – which all begins when fearful Great-aunt Olwen comes to stay . . .

Joan Aiken
MORTIMER'S CROSS

Illustrated by Quentin Blake

KNIGHT BOOKS
Hodder and Stoughton

Copyright © Joan Aiken Enterprises Ltd 1983
Illustrations © Quentin Blake 1983

First published by Cape/BBC 1983 as part of a collection of stories,
entitled *Mortimer's Cross*

This edition first published 1986 by Knight Books
Second impression 1986

British Library C.I.P.

Aiken, Joan
  Mortimer's cross.
  I. Title   II. Blake, Quentin
  823'.914[J]   PR6051.135

  ISBN 0-340-38847-1
  ISBN 0-563-20526-1 (BBC)

Printed and bound in Great Britain for
Hodder and Stoughton Paperbacks, a
division of Hodder and Stoughton Ltd.,
Mill Road, Dunton Green, Sevenoaks,
Kent (Editorial Office: 47 Bedford
Square, London, WC1 3DP) by
Richard Clay Ltd., Bungay, Suffolk.
Photoset by Rowland Phototypesetting
Ltd, Bury St Edmunds, Suffolk

1

It was a bitterly cold February day. The wind was as sharp as a nutmeg-grater. Arabel's socks, when Mrs Jones pegged them on the line, stopped steaming at once, and hung absolutely stiff, as if they had small stone feet inside them. Mr Jones, who was a taxi-driver, had to spray his taxi with anti-freeze before it would start; and besides that, he had to put pots of hot porridge and hot coffee inside the bonnet. Arabel Jones, even when she was indoors, wore so many sweaters that she looked like a football with two fair pigtails.

The only happy member of the family was Mortimer Jones, the raven. His black feathers were so thick and glossy that no amount of cold weather seemed to make him shiver.

But Mrs Jones kept saying, "Ohhhh, it is bitter! I can't manage to get warm, not any way. Can't stop shivering." Then, when Mr Jones came home for his lunch, she said, "My head isn't half hot, Ben. And my insides feel ever so all-overish. I believe I've been and gone and got the flu."

"Oh, bless me, Martha!" he said. "That's awkward, that is. You'd best get into bed, right off, and I'll stay home this afternoon and look after you. But what's to be done tomorrow? I'm booked to fetch a party of six from Bobbing Key, and take them to see the Radnor-Rumbury match at Twickenham."

"Why don't you ask Auntie Meg to come and look after Ma?" said Arabel, as Mrs Jones went slowly upstairs to bed, and Mr Jones waited for a kettle to boil, to make a hot water bottle.

"That's a real sensible notion, Arabel dearie," said Mr Jones, and as soon as his wife was settled with her hot bottle and two layers of quilts, he telephoned first the doctor, and then his sister Meg who helped run a pub on the edge of Wales.

The doctor said he couldn't come till tomorrow early. Rumbury Town was full of people with flu. He was run off his feet, and Mrs Jones was to stay in bed and take lots of hot lemon and aspirins. Mr Jones's sister Meg said she was sorry but she couldn't come; her cousin Gwen, who helped her run the pub, was in hospital with flu and a touch of pleurisy, so Meg had to manage the pub on her own.

"It's a terrible time," she said. "Everyone's got the flu, except the ones that haven't. Why don't you send for Aunt Olwen? *She'd* come like a shot. She *loves* looking after other people's houses, and if a flu germ came up to her she'd hit it with a broom handle."

"Yeah; I reckon I'll have to get her," said Mr Jones heavily. "Thanks, Meg."

"By the way," said Meg, "there's a box of clothes and toys Martha promised to let me have. For my Friends of Foxhounds Relief Society. I need it urgently for the sale on Thursday. D'you know if Martha sent it off?"

"I dunno," said Mr Jones. "I seem to remember her packing it up. I'll see. Goodbye, Meg."

Then he telephoned his Aunt Olwen in Bangor.

"That you, Ben?" said Aunt Olwen. "Yes, I'll come. Flu, Martha's got, has she? Humph! That's what comes of wearing nylons and that thin underwear. No more than to be expected. Time and again I've said so. Well, you'll all get it now, I daresay. First thing tomorrow morning I'll be with you. My neighbour Tom Griffith can bring me. Driving up to London anyway, he is, to see the football match at Twickenham. I'll be in Rumbury Town by breakfast time. And I'll bring sister Bronwen's clock that she left you when she passed on."

"I dunno as we've room for the clock –"
Mr Jones began, but his Aunt Olwen had
already rung off.

So it was arranged.

When Arabel heard that, instead of
cheerful talkative lively Aunt Meg, they
were to be looked after by her Great-aunt
Olwen, she let out a wail of dismay.

"Oh, Pa! Last time Great-aunt was here,
she put some stuff on my hair to stop it
tangling that made it set as hard as cement.
And she made me swallow five spoonfuls of
cod-liver oil before every *single* meal. And
she spent three days cleaning the house, and
two days scrubbing inside the teapot,
specially the spout, and then the spout came
away in her hand. And she switched off all
the switches in the house, so that everything
in the deep-freeze went mouldy. You said it
would be over your dead body if she ever
came here again."

"I know, dearie, but it'll be over your
ma's dead body if she *don't* come," said Mr
Jones, poking his fingers through his hair till

6

it looked like a bunch of windblown chrysanthemums.

"And Great-aunt Olwen's never even seen Mortimer, because we didn't have him last time she came," Arabel went on anxiously, looking at the raven, who had piled a foot-high mound of tea-bags on the lid of the washing-machine, and was trying to stand on his head on top of the pile. He was the wrong shape for standing on his head, and, each time he tried, he fell heavily on his

back, and the tea-bags flew all over the kitchen floor. They were getting rather dusty. Mr Jones supposed he ought to stop Mortimer, but he had too much else on his mind.

"It would certainly be a good thing if Aunt Olwen *didn't* see Mortimer, lovey," he said. "You don't suppose, just while she's here, that you could ask Mortimer to stop inside his box?"

Mortimer's box stood in a corner of the kitchen by the refrigerator. Auntie Meg had once brought it up, when she came on a visit, full of Worcester apples. Arabel and Mortimer both liked the box because it had MORTIMER'S CROSS stencilled on its side, and under that the letters H.A.R.R.I.S. A long time ago the box had held a lot of sockets, which were being delivered to the Hereford Admiralty Radar Research and Information Station, and then it had held empty beer-bottles, which the men who worked at the Mortimer's Cross Radar Station were taking back to the pub, and

then Auntie Meg had used it for apples.
Arabel said that the letters H.A.R.R.I.S.
stood for, *Hush! A Resting Raven's Inside, Ssh!*
Ever since the box had come into the house,
Mortimer had used it as a brooding-place.
At times when he was sulky, or gloomy, or
upset, or thoughtful, or wanted to remember
something, or digest his lunch, or just go to
sleep, he climbed into the box, and pulled
the four flaps down over his head.
Sometimes, in cold or wet weather, he stayed
there for hours.

Arabel looked thoughtfully at the box now, and said, "I could *ask* him. But the trouble is, if you ask Mortimer to do something, it mostly makes him want to do something else, just the opposite."

"You're telling me," said Mr Jones. "Oh well, have to hope for the best, I suppose." He did not *sound* at all hopeful.

Next day was colder than ever. Great-aunt Olwen arrived before breakfast. She and Mr Griffith had been driving all night, in his big old car that only went forty miles an hour. Mr Griffith said the roads were like frozen salad-oil. Great-aunt Olwen wore a black bugled dolman all covered with jet beads, a bonnet with forty shining black cherries on it, black high-button boots, and a big black shawl which covered her from head to foot, and made her look like a walking wigwam. She had an umbrella, and a chimney-sweep's brush, and a Gladstone bag, which contained six white aprons, an alarm clock, a flannel nightgown, an electric scrubbing-brush, a four-pound tin of

10

beeswax, a carton of Best Cardiff Scouring Powder, and a window-cleaning tool. They also had with them in the car Mr Griffith's St Bernard, Sam, and Great-aunt Olwen's sister Bronwen's grandfather clock, which was six feet high, so it was lucky the car was a big one. The mahogany case of the clock was decorated all over with brown and gold birds and fishes. The clock face had the sun, moon, stars, and a rainbow on it. Arabel thought it very beautiful. The clock's door swung open as Mr Jones and Mr Griffith were carrying it into the house, staggering rather, because it was so heavy. The clock door was three feet above ground level, where the clock's stomach might have been; inside could be seen a big brass pendulum, which swung slowly from side to side, and two large iron weights dangling on cords.

Mortimer, who had been sitting on the windowsill half-way up the stairs, half hidden by the curtain, stared very hard at the clock's inside. He was disappointed when Mr Jones shut the door and turned the key.

"Phew!" said Mr Griffith, wiping his forehead. "Good riddance to get rid of that, I'm telling you. Struck every blessed quarter

from Bangor to here; and a tick loud enough to drown nightingales. Where d'you want her, Ben?"

"Right here in the hall is the only place where there's room," said Mr Jones, who was anxious to settle his aunt and hurry off to pick up his customers in Bobbing Key. "And thank you kindly, Tom Griffith, for taking the trouble to bring it; not to mention my Auntie Olwen."

"No trouble," said Mr Griffith. "Coming up from Bangor anyway. But as for *that* one —"

Great-aunt Olwen had already stumped off upstairs, switching on her hearing-aid as she went. She did not notice Mortimer behind his curtain. But he was mightily interested in her hearing-aid, and peered at it as she went by.

Mr Griffith threw up his eyes, shook his head after Great-aunt Olwen, and hissed, "Proper cockatrice you've got there, my word! Make a pterodactyl go back and wipe its feet on the mat, *she* would. Wanted my

Sam to run behind the car, all the way from Bangor."

Mr Griffith's St Bernard was looking in the front door with great mournful St Bernard eyes. His ears, the size of dishcloths, hung down on either side of his face. "Said she wasn't used to travelling with a dog that size in the car, and if he was used to following tracks, he might as well follow ours."

"Is he used to following tracks, Mr Griffith?" asked Arabel.

"Follow a mosquito from here to the moon, dearie."

At this moment Mortimer came flopping down the stairs, and, after quietly edging close to Sam, suddenly took hold of the St Bernard's tail. There was a short, sharp scene. Then Mr Griffith and Sam went off to have breakfast at the Eggs-Quiz-It Snackbar, and Mr Jones hurried away to pick up his fares in Bobbing Key.

"You shouldn't have done that to Sam, Mortimer," said Arabel. "He was a visitor."

Mortimer took no notice. He was staring thoughtfully at the grandfather clock. But Mr Jones, knowing Mortimer's habits, had taken out the key and put it in his waistcoat pocket.

In a couple of hours, Great-aunt Olwen had the house turned upside down.

First she moved all the furniture in Mrs Jones's bedroom "so as to make it easier to get at the patient."

While she had four chairs, the laundry-basket, an electric heater, and a standard lamp piled on the wardrobe, which lay on its side, the front doorbell rang.

"I expect that's the doctor," said Arabel, peering into her mother's room over a barricade of furniture.

"What did you say, dear?" said Great-aunt Olwen, turning up her hearing-aid.

Great-aunt Olwen's hearing-aid consisted of a plug, which fitted her ear, a cord, which dangled round her neck, and, at the other

end of the cord, a little box with a battery
inside it and a grating on the front. It had a
switch like a radio so that the volume could
be turned up or down. The box was pinned
to Aunt Olwen's apron bib. When the
grating was turned towards a sound, Aunt
Olwen could hear it; but Arabel was
standing behind her great-aunt.

"Speak up, child!" said Great-aunt Olwen, turning up the hearing-aid a bit more.

"There's someone at the front door. I expect it's the doctor!" shouted Arabel, climbing over the wardrobe and coming round to the front of her great-aunt.

"No need to shout, child, I can hear you perfectly well. I'm not deaf! Answer the door then, will you, while I just hoover under your mother's bed," said Great-aunt Olwen, poking the nozzle of the vacuum cleaner under poor Mrs Jones.

Arabel climbed back over the wardrobe and went to answer the front door.

Outside was Dr McCaution, looking harassed.

"Mrs Jones, Number Six Rainwater Crescent, says she has flu," he muttered, looking at his list, which was as long as the trans-Siberian railway.

"Will you come upstairs, please?" said Arabel.

As the doctor went ahead of her up the

stairs he noticed the sound of the grandfather clock ticking. It had an exceptionally loud tick-tock, tick-tock, very slow and solemn; it sounded like an ostrich, with iron weights tied to its feet, crossing a hollow glass pavement. And Mortimer, sitting in front of the clock, was grumbling to himself vexedly between ticks, so what the doctor heard went like this:

"Tick. Nevermore. Tock. Nevermore. Tick. Nevermore. Tock. *Kaaark!*"

"Advise you to put a stop to *that*," said the doctor. "Disturbing for an invalid, very; in fact it's enough to *give* anybody flu – if not delirium tremens – just listening to it."

He was obliged to shove away the wardrobe lying on its side across the doorway of Mrs Jones's room; then he gazed round him in surprise. The bedroom was looking very upheaved; all the curtains, the bedcover, and the frilly skirts of the dressing-table were piled on the towel-rail; the carpet was rolled up, and every bit of furniture was on top of something else. Great-aunt Olwen had finished vacuuming (although she had not switched the cleaner off); she was about to scrub; Dr McCaution only just avoided putting his foot in a pail of hot soapy water.

"God bless my soul, ma'am, what's this, stocktaking day or judgement day?" said the doctor, putting a thermometer in Mrs Jones's mouth and taking her pulse.

"Cleanliness, young man, is next to

godliness," said Aunt Olwen.

"What the blue blazes is making that buzzing noise?" said the doctor.

As well as the noise of the vacuum cleaner, there was a harsh rattling buzz coming from one corner of the room.

"Oh, d-d-doctor! Maybe it's me! Maybe I've got the d-death-rattles," whimpered poor Mrs Jones, taking the thermometer out of her mouth and putting it into a cup of hot lemon which Arabel had brought her.

"Rubbish, Mrs Jones; it's coming from that Gladstone bag."

Great-aunt Olwen's bag stood near the door. She had not completely unpacked it yet, she had been so eager to get to the cleaning; had only taken out the beeswax, the window-cleaning tool, the scouring powder, and the first of her six white aprons. There was an unmistakable loud buzz coming from the bag. Aunt Olwen had not noticed it because her hearing-aid was not very good at distinguishing one buzz from another.

20

"Maybe it's a bomb," suggested Arabel.

Dr McCaution approached the bag with care. Then he turned it sharply upside down, scattering the contents.

"Mind what you do with other people's property, young man!" said Aunt Olwen.

The noise proved to have been Aunt Olwen's electric battery-operated scrubbing brush, which had been whirring away to itself all the way up from Bangor. Mr Griffith had not heard it, because the grandfather clock had been ticking so loudly. The scrubbing-brush did a kind of dance, all by itself, over the bare boards; then the battery ran out, and it stopped.

"There! I must have forgotten to switch it off, and now the battery's worn out," said Aunt Olwen. "Ben will have to get a new one. I'm *that* absent-minded, one of these days I'll forget to breathe."

Mrs Jones looked as if she hoped that day would come soon.

The doctor pulled the thermometer out of the cup of hot lemon and looked at it.

"You've got flu, Mrs Jones," he said, scribbling on his pad. "You have a temperature of a hundred and thirty-six. Take these pills eight times a day, stay in bed till I tell you to get up, and *complete* rest and quiet, please; no noise or disturbances. Invalids need a peaceful, relaxed atmosphere," he shouted at Aunt Olwen, who had fetched her window-cleaning tool and was squeaking it up and down the dressing-table glass. The vacuum cleaner was still roaring to itself, and Aunt Olwen's hearing-aid, turned up to full volume, was letting out a high whine. "Anybody can see *this* hasn't been touched for months," she muttered grimly, wiping the glass with a wash-leather, taking no notice of the doctor.

Now from downstairs there came a tremendous clanging chime. It went on and on, sixteen strokes for the four quarters, then ten strokes for the hour.

"Good gad, what's that?" said the doctor, looping his muffler round his neck.

"It's my husband's mother's grandfather

clock," whispered Mrs Jones faintly. "Aunt Olwen just brought it from Bangor."

"Worth a mint, that clock is," said Aunt Olwen with satisfaction. Even she had heard the chimes.

"It's louder than Concorde," said the doctor. "You could get middle-ear disturbance listening to it. Better stick a sock in its stomach while you've got illness in the house. See you tomorrow, Mrs Jones."

Great-aunt Olwen followed Arabel and the doctor downstairs because she wanted some mothballs to tuck in between the bedclothes.

Down in the front hall, the first thing she saw was Mortimer. He had pulled the piano-stool across the dining-room, out into the hall, and up against the clock; he had hoisted the coal scuttle on top of the stool, and was now standing on the coal, with his eye pressed to the keyhole of the clock door.

"What in the world is *that?*" said Great-aunt Olwen sharply.

Her voice startled Mortimer. The coal

scuttle was not very well balanced on the piano stool, and when Mortimer turned round, he and the scuttle fell off the stool, thumping heavily against the door of the clock, and strewing coal over the grey wall-to-wall carpet.

The clock began striking as if all the hours had been joined together between now and the year two thousand.

"Oh, mercy, mercy, what's happened, stop that awful noise!" wailed Mrs Jones from upstairs. "My head feels as if it's going to split in half like a coconut."

The doctor kicked the clock till it stopped striking, and then escaped from Number Six, Rainwater Crescent, shouting, "Get that prescription made up as soon as possible!"

Mortimer had fallen among the lumps of coal, and was just picking himself up. Disappointed in his plan for getting into the clock, he was now gazing very keenly at Great-aunt Olwen's hearing-aid.

"What's *that?*" said Great-aunt Olwen again. She had fetched a brush and pan, and was sweeping up the coal. She poked at Mortimer with the brush.

"That's Mortimer," said Arabel. "He's our raven."

"Raven, you call him? He looks to me like a black imp from the pit," said Aunt Olwen. "Into a bath he goes before I'm an hour older, or my name's not Olwen Gwladys Angharad Merlwyn Jones. Crawling with germs from head to toe, he is, without a shadow of doubt; no wonder Martha has flu, only surprising it isn't pleurisy, psittacosis, and Ponsonby's disease."

"Oh, please, I don't think Mortimer would like being bathed at all, he isn't used to that sort of thing," said Arabel.

"He'll be used to it soon," said Aunt Olwen ominously, making a grab for Mortimer.

In return he made a snatch for her hearing-aid, but only succeeded in unplugging the cord from the box holding the battery.

"You just wait, you Turk!" threatened Aunt Olwen.

Luckily, at this moment, Mrs Jones's sister Brenda rang the doorbell; Mr Jones had told her Martha had flu, and she had come to ask if there was any way in which she could help, apart from staying in the house, which she could not do, as her husband and two of her three daughters were coming down with flu too.

Great-aunt Olwen gave her the prescription to take to the chemist's, and she took Arabel along with her to carry the basket. Arabel did not want to go; she was anxious about Mortimer; but he had retired into his box, and she hoped he would be safe there. Great-aunt Olwen had not noticed him getting in.

Unfortunately, for lunch they had tomato soup and biscuits. Mortimer loved tomato soup. He came out of the box while Aunt Olwen was upstairs taking Mrs Jones some camomile tea. She had made it with ginger by mistake, and Mrs Jones didn't much fancy it.

"Please, Mortimer, I think it would be best if you got back into your box," Arabel said in a low voice.

Mortimer took no notice. He was drinking a cup of tomato soup, very splashily. And he wanted another look at Aunt Olwen's hearing-aid.

When Aunt Olwen came downstairs again she gave a sharp look at Mortimer. Then she filled a large tub with hot water and put it on the kitchen table. And she fetched soap, and the vacuum cleaner, and detergent, and bath brick, and a bottle of disinfectant, and a corkscrew, and a skewer.

"Now then, you!" she said grimly.

"Oh, *please* don't do whatever you're going to do to Mortimer!" cried Arabel in horror. "He won't like it a bit, truly he won't!"

"No nasty germy bird is going to stay in any house that *I'm* in," said Aunt Olwen, pressing her lips tight together.

First she vacuumed Mortimer from head to tail. Twice his head got stuck up the tube, and she hauled him out again by his feet; his feathers stood on end like the rays of the sun, and several of them came out. He was so stunned by this treatment that he had no breath even to protest; anyway most of his breath had been sucked out of him by the vacuum.

Then Great-aunt Olwen plunged Mortimer (whom she was holding by his neck and legs) into the tubful of hot, sudsy water.

There was a terrific commotion. Water and froth rained all over the kitchen. Upstairs, Mrs Jones called faintly, "Oh, help! Whatever is going on? Is it a Martian invasion? I think I'm going to have a spasm!"

Smothered in soap, Mortimer became too slippery to hold, and he burst upstairs like a

steam-propelled missile, leaving a trail of spray and feathers behind him. He did not generally use his wings for flying, but this was one of the times when he thought it best to do so.

In the kitchen, Great-aunt Olwen, re-plugging her hearing-aid, was saying, "He needn't think I'm finished with him yet; just wait till I get my hands on him again."

Mrs Cross, from down the road, had popped her head round the back door with a bunch of grapes for Arabel's mother. She said to Aunt Olwen, "Better let me bandage your hands first." Aunt Olwen was bleeding from several peck marks. "I'd leave that bird alone if I were you," advised Mrs Cross. "He's nothing but trouble."

Great-aunt Olwen had never been defeated yet; she was determined to deal with Mortimer and stop him spreading germs. As soon as she was bandaged, she followed him to the airing-cupboard, where he had taken refuge, and dragged him out from among the sopping towels.

"You're going to have a proper clean-up, whether you like it or not," she told him. She had refilled the tub with hot water and put on heavy cleaning-gloves; now she scrubbed Mortimer all over, working the soap in between his feathers with a corkscrew, cleaning his feet with a skewer, and rinsing them separately in a soup-plate full of Dyegerm. When Mortimer opened his beak to gasp "Nevermore!" she poked in a piece of soap the size of a butter-bean, and Mortimer swallowed it before he could stop himself; after that, whenever he opened his beak to say something, all that came out were clots of froth as big as ping-pong balls.

"That'll clean you up inside as well," Aunt Olwen said.

Mortimer became quite dazed by all this unexpected misfortune; he no longer even tried to grab Aunt Olwen's hearing-aid, but just endured what was happening to him. He had gone absolutely stiff, hunching his head down between his shoulderblades, and hugging his wings tightly to his sides. His

31

eyes were shut, so as to keep out the soap.

In the fracas the cord of Aunt Olwen's hearing-aid had broken, so she took off the whole contraption and put it on the dresser.

"Ben will have to mend it when he comes in," she said. "Now: that bird's a bit more fit to live in a decent house. Arabel, you take this old bit of towel and dry him; then he can go in front of the stove to finish off. Mercy sakes, look at the time; your mother ought to have had her pill two hours ago."

Aunt Olwen fetched her spare hearing-aid from her bag, and put on her third apron (two had already been used up); she threw the tubful of Mortimer's bathwater out the back door, where it immediately froze all over the concrete path. Then, still being a bit distracted by all the excitement of cleaning Mortimer, she filled Mrs Jones's hot water bottle with lemonade, and took her a cup of hot disinfectant with honey in it; and she gave Arabel fried celery and bacon with salad-cream on it for tea. Aunt Olwen was so hasty in all her actions that very often two or three of them got crossed over like this. She put on the spare hearing-aid back to front, with its grating pressed against her chest, so all she could hear was her own heart beating.

Mortimer did not want any tea, though Arabel offered him some bacon with salad-cream on it; he turned his head the other way. And when she came to sit by him in front of the warm stove, he opened his eyes, just for a moment, and looked at her almost as if he hated her.

He opened his beak, but all that came out was a ball of froth, so he shut it again. But

Arabel knew what he would have liked to say: *why didn't you stop that person doing those terrible things to me?*

"It wasn't my fault, Mortimer," Arabel whispered miserably. "I *did* warn you to stay in your box. And I did *try* to stop her."

Mortimer closed his eyes as if he didn't believe her.

Great-aunt Olwen went upstairs to give the guest room a thorough turn-out before making up a bed for herself with clean sheets.

When Mortimer was more or less dry, he climbed slowly and wearily into his MORTIMER'S CROSS box, and pulled the flaps down over him. Inside the box he had an old piece of blanket, which was comfortably covered with cake-crumbs and mouldy bits of cheese-rind, and dead leaves, and twigs, and snail-shells, and dried worms, and coke-can openers, and ice-cream papers, and other things he had collected at one time or another, besides an inch-thick layer of dust; he wrapped himself tight in

34

this blanket, and stuffed his head under his wing. He felt horrible; slimy and itchy between his feathers, damp and uncomfortable under his wings and tail; his feet were sore from the disinfectant, and his eyes stung from the detergent; the soap tasted disgusting in his beak; and even far down under his wing, his feathers smelt of Cleanol.

If there had been a prize going for the most miserable bird in Rumbury Town, Mortimer would certainly have won it.

Mr Jones became worried when he got back home (which was not very early, because after the football match, in which Radnor Forest won the Cup, he had to take his customers back to Bobbing Key). When he let himself in, he noticed at once that the house smelt frighteningly clean, of soap and detergent and beeswax and disinfectant; he could hear the loud gloomy tick of the grandfather clock, but, apart from that, no other sound at all.

"Hallo? Where is everybody?" he called.

His Aunt Olwen came out of the kitchen.

"Is that you, Ben? Martha's a little better; the doctor said her temperature was a hundred and thirty-six this morning, but it's only a hundred and three now. Don't go up to see her till you've had a good wash, and gargled with Dyegerm; you'll find a big bottle by the kitchen sink. I daresay the whole of outdoors is swarming with germs."

"Where's Arabel?" asked Mr Jones uneasily. "And – and Mortimer?"

"The child's in her room," snapped Aunt Olwen. "I told her to play with the button-box. At my age I can't have children underfoot when I'm trying to get the house cleaned up. As for the bird, he took himself off somewhere, I'm sure I don't know where. And the longer he stays out of sight, the better I'm pleased. Birds in the house, indeed! Now your supper's ready, Ben, so hurry up and eat it."

The supper Aunt Olwen had cooked for Mr Jones showed signs of her absentmindedness. Instead of stewing apples and grilling hamburgers, she had toasted the apples under the grill, and poached the hamburgers in hot water. Mr Jones ate them without grumbling. What else could he do? Someone had to look after his wife Martha while she had the flu. Afterwards he went up to see her. She was hot and feverish.

"The tick of that great clock downstairs goes through my head like a Laser Beam of Ancient Rome, Ben," she whispered fretfully. "And has it *got* to chime so often? It seems to keep ding-donging away every ten minutes. It's driving me clean dementiated. And where's Arabel? She hasn't been in to see me since tea-time. And what about Mortimer? He's ever so quiet. That's never a good sign, you know it isn't. I only hope he's not up to something."

Mr Jones hoped so too. He knew that when Mortimer was quiet, it did often mean that he was thoughtfully munching up the gas boiler, or dropping eggs off the top of the wardrobe, to see how many bounced, or pouring weedkiller into the television.

"I'll see what Mortimer's up to," he said, "and send Arabel to sit with you."

Arabel came to sit by her mother, but she was very pale and quiet.

"What's the matter, dearie?" whispered Mrs Jones. "Do you think you're sickening for the flu too?"

"No, Ma," said Arabel. "It's just that –" she gulped. "M-Mortimer won't speak to me. Or look at me."

"Why ever not? You've never quarrelled with him?" Mrs Jones was amazed.

"No, Ma. It's because Great-aunt Olwen washed him."

"*Washed* him?"

"And he thinks it was my fault."

"Oh my gracious cats alive!"

Downstairs, Mr Jones was having the same sort of conversation with his Aunt Olwen.

He had stopped the grandfather clock, at ten to seven, by taking the key from his pocket, unlocking the door, bringing the brass pendulum to a stop, and clipping the cords of the two iron weights together with a clothes-peg, so that they could not move up and down. Aunt Olwen watched all this with a disapproving eye.

"Never been known to stop, that clock hasn't," she said. "Even when my dear sister Bronwen, that was your mother, went to her rest. All the drive up from Bangor it went on ticking – as steady as Saturday. And now you have to stop it!"

"It's driving Martha crazy. And Mrs Walters from three doors down came to complain about the chime."

"Some people are never grateful," said Aunt Olwen, clamping her lips together.

Mr Jones peered through the slit in the box beside the fridge. There was Mortimer, a tight cocoon of greasy, crumby blanket, quiet as the stone inside a Victoria plum, with not a feather showing.

Rather cautiously, Mr Jones asked his aunt: "Has Mortimer – er – did he behave himself while I was out?"

"Behave himself? I should hope so,"

snorted Aunt Olwen. "No raven misbehaves himself in any house where I am! I gave him a good scrub, and disinfected him. Disgraceful state that bird was in! *Christmas-pudding crumbs*, I found, in among his feathers. Last year's, for all I know."

"You washed him?" said Mr Jones faintly. "Washed Mortimer?"

"Indeed I did. All over. Walking parcel of germs, that bird was. No wonder Martha caught the flu."

"Oh dear," said Mr Jones. It seemed wrong to complain since Aunt Olwen had come all this way from Bangor to look after them, but he did think that washing Mortimer might have been a terrible mistake.

On his way back upstairs he stopped by Mortimer's box once more.

"Er – I believe she meant it for the best, Mortimer, my boy," he said pleadingly. "I – I expect you'll feel the benefit of it in a few days."

Mr Jones did not observe that the

grandfather clock key fell out from his waistcoat pocket as he stooped over the box. Dead silence came from between the flaps. Not the faintest *Kark*, or whisper of *Nevermore*. Not so much as a bubble of foam, even.

2

Nobody slept well in the Jones' house that night. Mrs Jones tossed and turned in her fever; she twisted about in bed, and cried out, and dreamed that she was posting parcels full of foxhounds to the Hunt Master General, and that Mortimer was being chased by a pack of grandfather clock patients from the watch hospital on Rumbury Hill. Mr Jones slept on the sofa in the sitting-room, so as not to disturb his wife; his feet stuck out over the end, and were soon like lumps of ice. Arabel got out of bed as soon as her father had said goodnight to her, and spent the next eight hours making a huge pattern with shirt-buttons all over her bedroom floor. She cried a good

deal as she was doing it. Great-aunt Olwen
also slept badly, but that was because of her
alarm clock. It had a tremendously loud
ring, so that she could hear it even after she
had taken off her spare hearing-aid for the

night; and she set it to go off every hour, so
that she could go and look at Mrs Jones.
Every time the alarm went off, it woke
everybody else in the house too; those that
were asleep, that is.

"Why do you keep coming to look at me,
Aunt Olwen?" Mrs Jones whispered fretfully
at three in the morning. "I'm not likely to
run away!"

"Coming to see if you're all right, I am,"
said Aunt Olwen.

"Well, I'm *not* all right – I had a horrible
dream. Oh, my dear gracious – that reminds
me – "

"Reminds you of what?"

"I promised to send a parcel of clothes
and books and toys to Ben's sister Meg. For
her Friends of Foxhounds Relief Society
Sale – and she wants it by Thursday – I
meant to have sent it off two days ago, oh my
good heavens, and Meg is waiting for it, oh
dear, oh me – "

"Now don't get into a fidget, Martha, and
thrash about so," said Aunt Olwen. "Maybe

44

Ben posted it. And if he didn't, there's nothing that can be done at this time of night. If it's still there, I'll send it off for you in the morning."

"By express!"

"Very well, if you're so set on it," said Aunt Olwen, sucking in her mouth sourly. "Though why you should waste your money – or Ben's, rather – on friends of Megan Jones's foxhounds, I'm sure *I* don't know – "

"Downstairs," whispered Mrs Jones. "In the lounge, or maybe the kitchen. A big cardboard box. Addressed to Miss Jones at the Red Dragon, Mortimer's Cross."

"All right, all right, I'll see to it," grumbled Aunt Olwen. "I didn't get up at three in the morning to worry about Megan Jones's foxhounds society."

"You will send it the quickest way, won't you?"

"Yes, yes, if you're so set on it," said Aunt Olwen, and she went back to bed.

Next day Mr Jones found the atmosphere, and the breakfast, in Number Six, Rainwater Crescent so dismal that he went off to drive his taxi at half-past seven in the morning, and picked up a fare who wanted to be taken to Stratford-on-Avon. So he was away until after lunch. Arabel went back to her own room after breakfast, which was porridge with a lot of mysterious black things in it. Aunt Olwen had left the porridge cooking on the stove all night. Arabel wondered if the black things were lumps of coal. Politely, when Aunt Olwen wasn't looking, she put them in the sink disposal unit. She spent the morning going on with her button-pattern. She looked very pale and hollow-eyed.

Mrs Jones asked about her parcel at lunch time, when she was sipping a little broth, which tasted as if it had been made from Dark Tan shoe polish.

"Don't fret so, Martha, I sent it off express, just like you asked. Took it to that place on the corner, calls himself Johnny

Jardine's Do-or-Die Delivery Agency. He said he'd send a lad on a motorbike with it directly, and it would get there by tomorrow at latest. *Shocking* price it was – four pounds fifty! All for those friends of foxhounds. Ridiculous waste of cash, I call it,'' sniffed Aunt Olwen.

Mrs Jones was so relieved at hearing this, that she went to sleep quite peacefully, and when the doctor called her temperature had come down a little.

Mr Jones came home in the middle of the afternoon, and was pleased to hear that his wife had taken some broth. "And where's Arabel?'' he inquired.

"Still up in her room,'' said Aunt Olwen shortly.

Mr Jones went up to see his daughter. He discovered that, all across the floor of her room, using hundreds and thousands of shirt buttons, she had made an enormous pearly pattern that said I'M SORRY, MORTIMER, over and over, about eighty times.

"Do you think he'll understand that, Pa?" she said.

"Well – I dunno," Mr Jones said. He added, trying to sound hopeful about it, "Very likely he will. We never did ask him if he could read. I'll just fetch him up now, shall I, and we'll soon see."

He went downstairs again, into the kitchen, and came to a sudden stop.

"Aunt Olwen – where's Mortimer?"

"Don't ask *me!*" snapped his aunt. "Where would he usually be, at this time of day? Wherever that is, that's where he'll be!"

"He'd most likely be in his box; the one that used to stand here. Where have you put it, Aunt Olwen?"

And Mr Jones pointed to the space beside the refrigerator, where Mortimer's box usually stood.

"That box? Why, I put a bit of string round it and sent it off. Martha was on about it, like something possessed, at three o'clock in the morning."

"You sent if off?" said Mr Jones faintly. "Sent if off where?"

"Wherever the address on it said. *I* didn't address it, Martha did. To your blessed sister Megan's friends of foxes something society."

Mr Jones leapt towards the stairs, then stopped himself. He went into the sitting-room and lifted out a large box full of clothes from behind the sofa.

"Aunt Olwen – *this* was the box that ought to have been posted. See, it has Megan's address on a label."

"Well you don't have to hold it under my *nose*; I can *read*," said Aunt Olwen. "And you don't have to shout either, I'm not deaf! That's a daft place to leave a parcel, if you ask me, behind the sofa."

She was beginning to look rather fidgety.

"So you must have posted off *Mortimer*'s box. With him inside it!"

Arabel had come downstairs to see why her father was taking so long in fetching Mortimer. She arrived just in time to hear this. She went as white as a meringue.

"Oh, Pa!" she whispered. "What ever shall we do?"

"Well, now," said Mr Jones, "the first thing we must do is not get in a panic." He said this because he was fairly near panic himself. He knew how attached his daughter was to Mortimer. And he didn't want his wife upset. And she did get upset very easily.

He said, "We don't know for *sure* that

Mortimer was in that box. So first we'll have a good, quiet hunt all over the house. And the second thing is not to worry your Ma; we won't tell her about this, eh, till she's a bit better. And I daresay Aunt Olwen won't mind sending off the *other* box, as she's good at posting boxes," he addded rather coldly.

Aunt Olwen gave him an old-fashioned look, but she took the other box, put on her shawl and bonnet, and hurried off. Arabel noticed that there seemed to be something odd about Aunt Olwen's bonnet – most of the cherries seemed to be missing – but Aunt Olwen skewered it on her head and went off without observing this.

While she was out, Mr Jones and Arabel searched feverishly all over the house for Mortimer. It was easy to do this, because the house was now in such apple-pie order that even the spoons and forks were laid out in rows, like Olympic swimmers; and a large raven anywhere would have been perfectly conspicuous. But no raven was to be seen anywhere; not in the bath, nor the refrigerator, nor the clock, nor the oven, nor the deep-freeze; nowhere.

Aunt Olwen came back from Johnny Jardine's Do-or-Die Delivery Agency, saying, "Well, there's no call to get in such a fuss, Ben. The young man at the office has it down in his despatch book that the parcel I took him this morning was simply addressed to Mortimer's Cross, H.A.R.R.I.S. So that's where it'll go."

"But that's the Hereford Admiralty Research Station. What'll they do when they open a box and find Mortimer?"

"Don't ask me," said Aunt Olwen shortly. "One thing, they won't find any germs on him, that I do know. Look here! Look at my bonnet! What's happened to it? Where's all the cherries off it?"

Mr Jones didn't answer. He went to the telephone and asked for Directory Inquiries.

Aunt Olwen began mixing bran and raisins and chutney, muttering, "Martha needs building up, I'll make an apple crumble. Ben!" she called. "Ben! Where does Martha keep cooking-apples?"

"I want the number of Mortimer's Cross Admiralty Research Station, Hereford," Mr Jones told the operator. "In the larder," he called to Aunt Olwen.

"In the garden? That's a funny place to keep apples," said Aunt Olwen.

"Just wait a minute," said the operator to Mr Jones.

After he had waited quite a long time, the operator told him that it was a restricted number, and could not be given to ordinary members of the public.

"Who do you wish to contact at that number? And why do you want it?" she said.

"Because," said Mr Jones, "I have reason to believe that my raven, Mortimer, has been sent there by mistake."

"I beg your pardon? I didn't quite catch what you said?"

Mr Jones began to repeat what he had said, but was distracted by a crash and a loud shriek from the direction of the back door. "Oh blimey, *now* what," he muttered.

"Never mind, dear, I'll have to call you back," he said to the operator.

There was nothing in the kitchen to account for the crash and the shriek. But when Mr Jones looked outside the back door, he saw his aunt Olwen lying flat on the path. She had slipped on the sheet of ice that formed when she threw out Mortimer's bathwater, and it seemed highly probable that she had broken her leg.

"Don't you move, Aunt Olwen," said Mr Jones, gritting his teeth, "I'll just run next door and fetch Chris Cross. He's a strong lad, and with the two of us we'll soon have you off there."

Luckily Chris was at home, and he helped Mr Jones carry Aunt Olwen in and lay her on the sofa; then Mr Jones phoned for an ambulance, which said it would be there as soon as it could. People were falling down on sheets of ice all over Rumbury Town and the ambulances were running about like ants. Aunt Olwen sucked her mouth in furiously; she knew she could not blame anyone else

for the ice, since it was entirely her own
fault.

Mr Jones packed a bag with his aunt's
flannel nightdress and toothbrush, since it
seemed almost certain that she would have
to spend the night in hospital. He did not
put in her six white aprons or the electric
scrubber or the window-cleaning tool.

"Mind you put in my spare hearing-aid that

you mended, Ben," she said. "I daresay those young things of nurses all mumble so you can't hear what they say, and I like to be on the safe side."

But the spare hearing-aid could not be found. "I left it on the dresser, after I mended it," said Mr Jones. "Maybe Arabel moved it. Arabel, dearie! Where are you? ARABEL!!"

But no answer came from Arabel. After a minute or two Mr Jones realised, with utter horror, that he was alone in the house with two people, one with flu, and the other a broken leg, while his daughter and his raven were both missing.

Where, meanwhile, *was* Arabel?

While Mr Jones was out fetching Chris Cross, there had been a ring at the front doorbell. Arabel went to the door and found Mr Griffith. His large car was parked just along the road with Sam the St Bernard looking out.

Mr Griffith said, "Called to inquire if your Great-auntie wanted a ride back to Bangor? I'm just on my way."

"Oh, I *wish* she did," said Arabel sadly. "But she's broken her leg and has to have it mended."

Mr Griffith brightened up when he heard that Aunt Olwen would not be his passenger. He said, "Your Auntie Meg mentioned something about a box of clothes for her Friends of Foxhounds Society. (Can't think why foxhounds need friends, St Bernards get on all right without, eh, Sam?) I said, if your ma hadn't posted the box already, I'd take it, as I'll be going through Mortimer's Cross."

"You *will*?" said Arabel, all excited. "It's all right about the box, Mr Griffith, Aunt Olwen sent it off. But – if you're going through Mortimer's Cross – could you take *me*? I can stay the night with Auntie Meg – "

"Want you out of the way, do they, while your Ma's sick?" said Mr Griffith.

"Sensible, that is. Wrap up warm, then, and come along."

Arabel went into her mother's room to say she was going to Mortimer's Cross with Mr Griffith. But Mrs Jones was asleep and Arabel didn't like to wake her.

Then she called through the back door to Great-aunt Olwen, "I'm going to look for Mortimer, Aunt Olwen, with Mr Griffith."

But Great-aunt Olwen's hearing-aid was facing away from Arabel. She did not hear the message.

Arabel put her nightdress, and three ginger biscuits, which were Mortimer's particular favourites just then, into a little bag.

"All set?" said Mr Griffith. "You best hop in the back with Sam. I don't hold with young 'uns in the front seat."

He let off his handbrake and rolled away, just as Mr Jones came back with Chris Cross.

Arabel did not in the least mind going in the back seat with Sam. He was so large and

warm that it was like leaning against a live
haystack. His ears hung down on either side
of her, and she fell fast asleep, curled up
against him, and slept all the way to
Mortimer's Cross.

When she woke, it was because Mr
Griffith was shaking her.

"Show a leg, dearie! Dead to the wide, you
were. Here we are, and there's your Auntie
Meg."

Auntie Meg, who was round-faced and blue-eyed, and had black curly hair, seemed surprised but pleased to see Arabel.

"Ben never said anything about sending you, lovey," she said. "Company for me,

you'll be, while Gwennie's in hospital. Nice, that is!"

"I can't stay for long, Auntie Meg," Arabel said. "I just came because Mortimer got sent here by mistake, and I thought you might know where he was."

"Mortimer?"

"Our raven."

"Got sent to me?" Auntie Meg looked more and more puzzled. "Here," she said, "you'd best come inside, it's freezing and blowing like the day of judgement, and starting to snow, too. Come along in, Mr Griffith, and take a drop of my elderberry wine."

Mr Griffith said he didn't mind, and Arabel better watch out where she walked, the ground was like frozen spring onions. It was the middle of the night; Mr Griffith had taken a very long time over the drive, because the weather was so nasty.

"Now," said Auntie Meg, when they were in front of a roaring fire, Mr Griffith with the elderberry wine, Arabel with hot blackcurrant juice, and Sam with a bone. "Now what's all this about Mortimer being sent here?"

"You remember that box, Auntie Meg, that you once brought us some apples in?"

After a bit of reminding Auntie Meg said, "Oh yes, it was one of those Admiralty boxes, wasn't it. We get a lot of them here, the lads from the radio station bring back the beer empties in them."

"Well, yesterday, by mistake, Great-aunt Olwen sent Mortimer to you in that box. Didn't you get a box with a raven in it, by motorbike messenger?"

"I got a box with the clothes in it that your Ma sent . . . No, wait a minute, there was another box, that's right," said Auntie Meg. "But it wasn't for me, it was addressed to the radio station; I told the boy to take it on up the hill."

"Oh, then that's where he'll be!" cried Arabel joyfully. "Oh please, can I go up there now, Auntie Meg?"

"Well, now, hold on, dearie, it's a bit late

to go knocking people up and asking if they've got your raven. Suppose we wait till morning; then I'll give Commander Popjoy a tinkle; heart of gold that man has; always one for a laugh; if your bird's up there, Billy Popjoy will soon have him tracked down for you."

"But it's snowing, Auntie Meg," said Arabel doubtfully. "Suppose Mortimer's out in the snow somewhere?"

"Bless us, child, he's got some sense, hasn't he? Find himself a place to shelter, he will, sure as you're born," said Auntie Meg stoutly. "Now, let's all get a bit more sleep, shall we?"

Mr Griffith said he reckoned he'd doss down at Meg's for the rest of the night, if she'd no objection, as it was now snowing like a busted duvet, and he didn't fancy being frozen stiff as a haddock on the way to Bangor. So he went to sleep in Gwen's room.

3

Arabel, having slept such a lot in the car, woke up first, next morning, and could hardly contain herself till the others were awake. As soon as it was light she began looking out of the window, to see if she could see Mortimer anywhere.

She did not see Mortimer, but she did see the Admiralty Research Station.

The snowstorm had ended, and all the countryside was buried in a foot-deep layer of white, very thick and clean. At least that should make it easy to find Mortimer, Arabel thought, seeing he's so black.

Ice was everywhere, too, dangling in glittering points from trees and door-handles and fences and telegraph wires.

The Admiralty Research Station consisted
of a dozen low concrete huts, which were
now up to their eaves in snow and looked
like white pillows scattered about on the
hilltop. Then, among them, were three
enormous radar scanners the size of huge
circus rings tilted up sideways towards the
sky. They were curved and white, like
outsize soup plates, and they swung about
majestically, this way and that, exactly the

way that Great-aunt Olwen did when she was tilting her head, trying to catch what somebody said to her.

"Coo!" said Arabel to Sam the St Bernard, who was on the window-seat beside her. "I believe they're listening, Sam. I wonder what they are listening *to?*"

Sam didn't know, but Mr Griffith, who had come to fetch Arabel to breakfast, told her that the great screens were listening to messages from round the other side of the world, and goodness knows where else.

"Supposing Martians was coming from outer space, or moon-people, or flying saucers, those things would catch the sound of 'em far away, long before your ears or mine could."

"Coo," said Arabel again, and then he went to eat the hot porridge that Auntie Meg had made; it was much better than Aunt Olwen's with the black lumps in it.

After breakfast Auntie Meg was on the point of phoning Commander Popjoy when he arrived. He was a tall, bony, smiling man with a bright pink face and a shock of yellow hair, and he wore shiny crackly leggings and a dark-blue waterproof, and hanging over that was a pair of binoculars on a leather strap.

"Wonderful weather for bird-watching!!" he said. "Just on the way down I've seen a Snowy Boomerang, and a Jersey Cowfinch,

two Arctic Snippets, and what I'm almost
certain was a Great Western Night-Rail."
Then he and Meg hugged one another, and
he said, "Good morning, ducky," and she
said, "Good morning, Billy, bach,"; it was
plain that they were very fond of one
another. Aunt Meg said, "Billy and I are
going to be married as soon as Gwennie's
out of hospital." Then she said, "My niece
Arabel wants to speak to you, Billy, but first,
what brings you down to the Red Dragon so
early? It's not opening time!"

"Hoped I could use your phone," he said.
"All our lines at the station are down;
they're so iced over that the wires have
snapped off. And I'm worried about the
radio tower; the guy-cables are iced over too:
thousands of pounds of ice there must be,
dangling on those cables. Lucky it's calm
just now. Suppose a wind starts up, before
the sun melts the ice . . . If just *one* of those
cables was to snap from the weight of ice, it
might unbalance that tower."

"Dear to goodness!" shivered Aunt Meg.

She glanced up the hill at the radio tower, an immensely tall steel mast; it stood among the radar scanners like a bamboo among mushrooms. "Would the tower hit this house if it fell?"

"No, but it might hit your old barn. Is there anything valuable in there?"

"Not a thing, but there was three hippie-looking fellows hanging around it yesterday at tea-time. I told them to be off with themselves; they were a rascally-looking lot. I said that was where I kept the mad bull, but I don't know if they believed me."

"But what does your niece want to ask?" said Commander Popjoy kindly.

"Oh, please," said Arabel, "did my raven, Mortimer, get sent to your station yesterday by mistake? In a box that said Mortimer's Cross on it?"

"Well, we get dozens of boxes every day that say Mortimer's Cross on them," Commander Popjoy told her. "A lot did come yesterday, with valves and trivets and sprockets and gambrels in them. They haven't been unpacked yet. Would you know your box if you saw it?"

"Of course I would," Arabel was beginning, when Mr Griffith had a bright idea.

"Have you anything on you that belongs to Mortimer?" he inquired. "Like, as it might be, a leg-band, or a shed feather?"

Arabel did have a shed feather; several, in fact. She had picked them up from the kitchen floor after Great-aunt Olwen had finished bathing Mortimer.

She pulled some bent shiny black bits from her cardigan pocket.

"We'll give them to Sam to sniff and see if he can't run your bird to ground."

But Mr Griffith's plan did not work. When Sam was given the feathers to sniff, his response was to give a gloomy howl, retreat to a far corner, and huddle there with his paws over his face.

"I'm afraid he seems to have taken a dislike to your bird," said Mr Griffith, very disappointed.

70

"Never mind," said Commander Popjoy. "I've got a little bird-scanner; my own invention as a matter of fact," he added proudly. "We'll go up to the station and see what we can find."

"Can we go right away?" Arabel begged.

First, however, Commander Popjoy wanted to phone the big Admiralty station at Severn-side, to warn them that his tower was in a dangerous state, and ask them to send over some hot-air generators to melt the ice off the steel guy-ropes before the strain of the weight got too much, and one of the stays snapped, and the tower fell over. Luckily the Red Dragon phone was still working and he was able to send his message. Then Aunt Meg thought she had better call Mr Jones to say that Arabel had arrived safely at Mortimer's Cross. He sounded quite frantic with relief, when she did so, as he had spent the night phoning the police, the hospitals, and the fire-service to ask where his daughter had got to, and none of them had been a bit helpful. "Tell Arabel her Ma's much better," he shouted, "and Aunt Olwen's in hospital, and I'll come and fetch Arabel as soon as I can." Then he lowered his voice and asked, "Is Mortimer there?"

"We don't know yet," said Aunt Meg.

"Well – " said Mr Jones, "I do *hope* he's there, I'm sure, because Martha doesn't know he's lost yet, and she keeps asking for him; got a fancy to hear his voice, she says she has, don't ask me why, got an idea that it would help her to get better if she could only hear him grumbling 'Nevermore' in that way he does."

"Oh dear," said Meg. "Well, we'll see what we can do, Ben; we're just going to look for him now as a matter of fact."

Then the whole party, Arabel, Mr Griffith, and Aunt Meg (who was free to leave the pub because it wasn't opening time yet) piled into Commander Popjoy's Land-Rover, and he drove them, slithering from side to side, up the snowy track to the Radar Station. Sam stayed at the pub; since sniffing

Mortimer's feathers he had been in a very gloomy frame of mind.

Aunt Meg had lent Arabel a pair of gumboots which were much too big for her, but even so the snow came over the tops of them when she got out of the truck, so Commander Popjoy carried her into an enormous storage shed. Inside it were about a thousand boxes, all labelled MORTIMER'S CROSS H.A.R.R.I.S.

"Oh my goodness!" Arabel said in dismay, gazing round. "What a lot of boxes! Still, if Mortimer's here, maybe he'll hear us. . ." She opened her mouth as wide as it would go, and called, "Mortimer! Are you in here?"

"Not *too* loud, ducky," warned Commander Popjoy. "We don't want to start a lot of vibrations. Let's see what my scanner will do."

He pulled out of his anorak pocket a little black box, and opened it up. Inside was a little fan-shaped vane, made of grey pearly plastic, which began to twirl round and

round when he pressed a button; and the
box began to make a little quiet noise, *cheap-
cheap-cheap-cheap-cheap.*

"Well now, fancy!" said Auntie Meg.
"Isn't that clever, Billy bach! Can it tell one
kind of bird from another?"

"Well, it knows about size," said Commander Popjoy. "It makes a different noise for a thrush from what it would for a Whooping Swan. And it can spot any bird within a range of five hundred yards."

He began walking up and down beside all the ramparts, and stacks, and walls, and rows, and piles of boxes that said MORTIMER'S CROSS. He did this for quite a long time, and they all watched him. It was bitter cold, even inside the storage hangar.

Then Commander Popjoy's box began to go *twit-twit-twit-twit-twit*.

"It's picked something up," said the Commander. "We're getting warm."

He moved towards a box that was right up on top of a stack, with its flaps open. The *twit-twit-twit* grew louder. Commander Popjoy lifted down the box and looked inside.

"It's empty," he said, puzzled and disappointed. "But it seems to have an old blanket and some dried worms in it."

"Oh, then that *is* Mortimer's box," Arabel cried joyfully. "He must have got out of it and be walking round somewhere."

"*Twart, twart, wargle-wargle*," said the Commander's bird-scanner.

"It seems to get louder towards the door," said Billy Popjoy.

The whole party went outside again. Mr Griffith carried Arabel through the snow. Now they were among the great radar screens, which looked as big as town halls when you were right beside them; and the tremendously tall radio mast, built of dark-grey steel struts, towered high, high over their heads. The steel guy-ropes that tied it to the ground stretched away in all directions like the strands of a spiderweb. The ropes flashed with ice, which hung from them in a lacy glittering fringe.

"*Whatever* you do, don't touch those ropes," warned Commander Popjoy. Then he suddenly let out a yell of rage. "Who's pinched the lead off my radar scanners?"

"Lead, Billy bach?" said Aunt Meg. "What lead?"

"There isn't any! It's all gone," he said furiously. "All three of those screens ought to have lead backing. And someone's been and peeled it off them as if they were perishing oranges!"

"Pricey stuff, lead," said Mr Griffith, shaking his head. "Fetch dear knows what an ounce in Bangor Market, it do. Maybe it was those three rascally chaps you saw, Miss Megan."

But Arabel bit her lip anxiously. Eating the lead backing off radar screens was just the kind of thing Mortimer might take it into his head to do; particularly if he were feeling upset.

Now, suddenly, the bird scanner's *wargle-wargle* changed to a *crawk-crawk-crawk, wheeeeeee!* and, following its prompting, Commander Popjoy moved towards his radio tower and stood looking up.

They all looked up.

Arabel's heart almost froze inside her.

Mortimer the raven was about three-quarters of the way up the mast, climbing steadily by beak and claw, hoisting himself up from strut to strut. He was so far up that he looked quite tiny, but there was no doubt that it was Mortimer; Arabel was certain of it the minute she saw him.

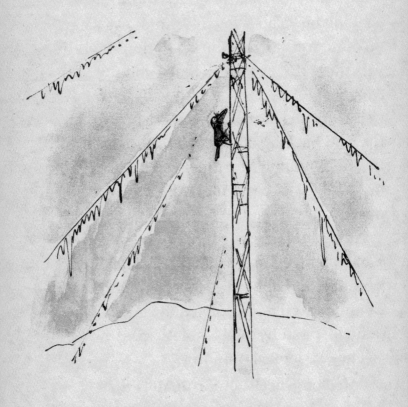

And the bird-scanner was now going *croop-croop-croop-croop-croop*.

"Merciful cats alive!" whispered Commander Popjoy, staring up through his binoculars. "A raven. *Corvus corax*. Or is it *rhipidurus*? No, I fear it is the common *corax*, but an uncommonly fine, large specimen, to be sure. But why, in the name of the purple pyramid, does it choose to climb up my radio mast?"

"Mortimer!" called Arabel gently. "We would rather you *didn't* climb Commander Popjoy's tower, if you don't mind. Could you come back down now, and climb it some other time?"

She did not dare call very loud. And Mortimer probably did not hear her. At any rate, he took no notice, but went on climbing, rather faster; he was very nearly at the top now.

Far away, at the bottom of the hill, some Admiralty hot-air machines could be seen arriving. They were bright red generators, mounted on wheels; unfortunately they found it quite impossible to get up the icy, slippery hill. A lot of men jumped out of them and began desperately shovelling sand on to the road.

Now Mortimer was right at the top of the tower. He must have had a fine view from up there, Arabel thought; and apparently he thought so too. He hung rather nonchalantly sideways, and stared, turning his head round and round, like the scanners; stared at the white world stretching away for hundreds of miles in all directions.

"What does that tower *do*, Mr Popjoy?" Arabel asked. "What is it for?"

"Why – why, it's used to send messages, ducky; it catches waves in the air, up there, and bounces them a bit farther."

"Could it send a message to Mars?"

"Very likely, if there was anybody on Mars to hear the message. Do you think your raven will fly down quite soon now?" said Commander Popjoy, his voice almost breaking with strain. "The way he's swinging about up there, I'm not sure if – "

"Mortimer!" called Arabel, a little louder. "We'd like you to come down now, please!"

Mortimer glanced down at her. Then he opened his beak. First of all a bubble of soap – the last – came floating up out of his throat; and after it had drifted away, with all the power of his raven lungs, Mortimer yelled "NEVERMORE!" – sounding as if he hoped and expected that his voice would carry all the way to Mars.

There was a short pause.

Then one of the steel cables snapped, with a musical clang. The tower staggered slightly, like a person who has been hit with a banana peel. After that, in very quick succession, the other cables began to part and snap, as the tower jerked about, its weight being pulled first one way and then another by the tension of the cables that remained.

"*Down!* Get down on your faces!" yelled Commander Popjoy. "If one of those cables hits you, it'll cut you in half like Dutch cheese!"

He threw Arabel and Meg down in the
snow and lay protecting them with his arms.
Up above, they could hear the cables
clanging away as if somebody were plucking

a huge mandolin: *twing! twang! twong! twang! twing!*

Then there was another moment's silence; then a great shuddering wrenching grinding groaning *scrunch*, as if a giant's tooth had been pulled out, and the whole radio tower fell over on its side like a forest tree, neatly missing two of the concrete sheds, squashing a generator truck, and slicing Auntie Meg's barn in half like a pumpkin.

It took a long, long time to clear up the mess. Luckily nobody had been hurt. Arabel, Meg, and Mr Griffith didn't stay for the tidying-up; they reckoned that they were more nuisance than help, and that it was best to get out of the way; specially as Mortimer, rather surprised by what had happened, came floating down out of the air to land on Arabel's shoulder.

"Oh, *Mortimer!*" she said. "Do you know what you've done?"

But Commander Popjoy, always a fair

man, said, "Eh, well, don't blame the bird too much; after all, it wasn't his fault that the cables were iced over." So Arabel gave Mortimer a ginger biscuit, which he munched with a thoughtful air. And when, later, it was discovered that a gang of three lead-thieves, known throughout North Wales as the Leadwaiters, had been trapped in Meg's barn by a tremendous tangle of steel struts, together with all the lead from the radar screens that they had been going to load on to a truck, the Commander was quite pleased and obliged to Mortimer.

Mr Jones came up to Mortimer's Cross next day. By then it had started raining, and was much warmer, and the snow was melting splashily away.

"How's Great-aunt Olwen, Pa?" Arabel asked, after they had said a loving goodbye to Auntie Meg and were driving away from the Red Dragon, with some more apples, and Mortimer back in his own box, blanket and all; the Commander had kindly brought it down to the pub when he came to take the lead thieves into custody.

"Your Great-aunt Olwen," said Mr Jones, "is being driven back to Bangor by your cousin Stephen; she's going to stay with your Aunt Lily till the plaster cast is off her leg."

Poor Aunt Lily, thought Arabel; but she said, "Who's looking after Ma, then?"

"Miss Cross from next door. She'll be there till we get home. And then I'll stay at home till Ma's better."

"That'll be nice," said Arabel. She leaned against Mr Jones, sucking her finger, all the way home. "Don't you think you're too old to suck your finger?" said Mr Jones. "Yes," said Arabel, and went on doing it.

When they got back to Rainwater Crescent, Mrs Cross greeted them with a broad smile. "Martha's had an egg for her tea, and she's feeling quite perkyish."

Arabel went up to see her mother.

"Look, Ma! I went to visit Auntie Meg all by myself, with Mr Griffith, and she gave me this blue sweater, made from Welsh sheep's wool. And we found Mortimer, and *he's* feeling better too."

"Was he lost, then? Where is he now?" said Mrs Jones. "I've a fancy to hear his voice."

Arabel went to find Mortimer. He was looking at the buttons in her room. After a long, thoughtful stare, he ate quite a number

of them. Then he hopped into Mrs Jones's room and croaked at her quietly two or three times: *Kaark*. "That's right, Mortimer, then," she said weakly.

Mortimer stood staring about the room as if he had forgotten something.

"What's the matter, Mortimer?" asked Mr Jones in a hearty voice, coming into the room.

All the family were being rather extra polite to Mortimer, as if he were a visitor they didn't know very well.

Mortimer appeared to remember what it was he had forgotten. He went downstairs quite fast – flop, scramble, thump, hop – and dragged the umbrella-stand across the front hall to the grandfather clock (the hands of which still stood at ten minutes to seven).

The door of the clock was open, because Mr Jones had never been able to find the key after it fell out of his waistcoat pocket. Mortimer clambered speedily up and down the umbrella-stand, fetching all his things – the dried worms, some of the buttons that had said I'M SORRY MORTIMER, the cake-crumby blanket, the snail-shells, some ginger biscuits – and dropped them inside the clock. When they were all in, he clambered in himself and squeezed down on top of them. It was a tight squeeze, for Mortimer was, as Commander Popjoy had said, a fine large specimen of a raven. But at last he had crammed himself down to the bottom of the clock. There he sat on top of his treasures – which also included the clock key, twenty black cherries off Aunt Olwen's bonnet, and her spare hearing-aid.

Arabel felt sure that he was wondering if his message had got to Mars.

If you have enjoyed reading this book you may like to read some more BBC/Knight titles:

JOAN AIKEN

ARABEL AND THE ESCAPED BLACK MAMBA

Mortimer was spearing his forty-ninth crisp when he hit the milk bottle which was standing on the table beside Chris. It fell to the floor and broke . . .

"There's a milk-vending machine by the dairy in the High Street," Chris said. "I'll go out and get some more."

"Ma said you were not to go out and leave me," said Arabel. "I'll come too."

What seems like a straightforward errand soon becomes another wonderful adventure for these Jackanory favourites.

BBC/KNIGHT BOOKS

JOAN AIKEN

THE BREAD BIN

With a neat wriggle, Mortimer slid from
Arabel's grasp, and climbed on to one of her
skates. Then he half spread his wings and gave
himself a mighty shove-off . . .

''Oh quick, stop him, stop him!' said Arabel . . .

''Stop that bird!'' shouted Auntie Brenda . . .

Taking a pet raven to a roller-skating rink
doesn't sound like a very sensible idea. But
Arabel's mother considers it a lot more
sensible than leaving Mortimer alone in the
house! And so begins another hilarious
adventure for Arabel and Mortimer.

BBC/KNIGHT BOOKS

JOAN EADINGTON

THE WORLD OF JONNY BRIGGS

"Surely I didn't hear the word RABBIT
HUTCH?" Jonny Brigg's mother said
accusingly. "Surely no one is hinting at the
presence of a RABBIT around this place?"

But this is exactly what Jonny Briggs is hinting
at, though he hadn't meant his mam to
overhear! And that's not the only thing he's
keen to complicate life with; his sudden
interest in making gingerbread men and kites
is bound to bring chaos – and fun – to the lives
of those around him . . .

Also by Joan Eadington:
JONNY BRIGGS AND THE SILVER PARTY

BBC/KNIGHT BOOKS

JOHN GRANT

LITTLENOSE AND TWO-EYES

Littlenose needed to concentrate. He had
passed the first three tests, but before his
name could be added to the tribe's roll of
Junior Hunters, he had to face the final, most
difficult test: Hunting the Grey Bear.

There was no time to play with Two-Eyes, his
pet mammoth – he even tried to send him
away! But luckily for Littlenose, Two-Eyes
wasn't easily put off.

This new collection of stories will delight
Littlenose's many friends.

BBC/KNIGHT BOOKS